NEON PRIME

Laura Shenton

NEON PRIME

Laura Shenton

Iridescent Toad Publishing

Iridescent Toad Publishing.

Cover by Louis Bulaso.

First edition. ISBN 978-1-9163478-2-3

Chapter One

Neon Prime was a city of contrasts, where towering skyscrapers laced with fluorescent light reached into the smog-filled sky, glowing in the blood-red horizon. In the air, hover-cars zoomed past, leaving shimmering trails behind them, while below, streets thrummed with restless energy. A delicate yet unspoken tension gripped the metropolis, binding its residents in a strained dance of survival.

Humans and Zarrons co-existed in the city, but just barely. The Zarrons, with their advanced technology, had long established themselves as masters of invention and power, but never quite as rulers. The humans, ever resilient, stood their ground, refusing to be outdone despite the Zarrons' clear edge. The uneasy partnership that formed the backbone of the planet's governance had kept peace, but it was a brittle peace, always on the verge of breaking.

Zyra moved through the crowds like a shadow, wearing a skirt and bodice made of dark reinforced synthetic leather that clung to her form, tailored to both accentuate her lithe physique and allow for maximum movement. The sleek material of her outfit shimmered faintly under the neon lights, its subtle sheen hinting at the concealed armour woven into its fibres.

Her striking pink skin gleamed, and her long green hair flowed behind her, catching the subtle breezes stirred by hover-cars passing overhead. Her eyes, always scanning, took in the hurried steps of both humans and Zarrons moving through the city. While there was no outward aggression, she could sense the thin veneer of civility between them. In the clashing gazes and in the quick, averted eyes of those trying to avoid conflict, the division was clear.

Zyra's right arm whirred softly with every motion, a glistening metallic green prosthetic that shimmered under the city's vibrant lights. Little did the humans know that the limb was Zarron-crafted, its sleek joints and hidden strength far exceeding anything their own technology could create.

As she flexed her hand absently, the artificial sinews responded with a precision that no human could match. It felt as natural to her as her own flesh. However, it served as a permanent reminder of her origins and the purpose for which she had been created.

Zyra wasn't fully human, and she wasn't fully Zarron. She was a hybrid, a rare mix of both species – crafted by the Zarrons to be a sleeper agent hidden within human society. She had been designed to embody the enhanced abilities of a Zarron, and to blend seamlessly with the humans, awaiting activation. And now, after years of living as a human, of building a life within the city of Neon Prime, that time had come.

The coded message blinked in her neural interface, its frigid, insistent beat reinforcing the imperative nature of her mission – a mission she had long tried to forget. The words of Commander Vohr echoed in her mind, his tone detached and cold, as it always was:

"Meet me at the designated location. We have much to discuss. Do not delay. The time has come for you to prove your loyalty."

Loyalty. The word churned uncomfortably in Zyra's gut. To whom did she owe this loyalty? To the Zarrons who had created her? Or to the humans who unknowingly accepted her? Neon Prime, with all its faults, had become her home. The people – flawed, stubborn, and endlessly resilient – had eased their way into her life in ways she hadn't been anticipating. In her time as a human-employed enforcer for the city's security forces, she had made connections. Friends, even.

Dane, her human colleague, was one of those connections. A pragmatic man with a sharp mind and sharper instincts, he had been her partner on the force for years. The trust they had built made Zyra's predicament all the more difficult to stomach.

She sighed, her gaze falling to the pistol holstered at her side. It hummed faintly, its sturdy black frame a perfect fusion of technology. Her fingers brushed against it – a reassuring weight she had relied on countless times in the line of duty. Now though, it felt heavier than usual.

As she turned to head down an alleyway, leaving the noise of the main streets behind, her thoughts spiralled back to Commander Vohr. His presence loomed over her like a dark cloud – firm clarification of her Zarron-defined purpose on Neon Prime. Commander Vohr had overseen her creation, crafted her into what she was, and he had always been clear about one thing: there was no room for rebellion, no room for defiance. The Zarrons would not tolerate insubordination.

Zyra's hand tightened around her pistol as she walked deeper into the alley. She had no choice but to go to Commander Vohr. If she didn't, he would send someone less patient, less forgiving. Zyra knew what happened to Zarron agents who defied their orders. But still, the thought of facing Commander Vohr again, of standing before him and being schooled on what she was supposed to be, filled her with an overwhelming sense of dread.

A part of her yearned to believe there was more to her existence than being a mere weapon for her creator.

Chapter Two

The underground levels of Neon Prime were a forgotten maze of rusted steel and flickering signs, still firmly held together by the city's ancient infrastructure. The air down here was heavier, laden with the scent of oil and damp, a constant reminder that not everyone in Neon Prime lived among its neon-lit glory.

Zyra's steps were quiet as she moved through the crowd. In this part of the city, no one made eye contact with anyone else. This was the place for people with secrets. Outcasts, criminals, rebels – those who lived on the fringes of society. Down here, they were all the same: all hiding something.

Zyra blended into the shadows as easily as she did into the crowd. Her enhanced senses – her Zarron-instilled instincts – were on high alert, the tension trickling through her veins.

The humans and Zarrons might pretend to co-exist above ground, but here, on the lower levels, even that pretence was absent. It was everyone for themselves.

Zyra approached a decrepit warehouse, its once-glimmering metallic walls now faded and streaked with rust. It stood at the edge of the district, tucked away behind a crumbling labyrinth of industrial waste. Her heart pounded as she neared the entrance, her steps slowing as she prepared herself for the encounter awaiting her inside. This wasn't to be just another mission briefing, but a reckoning.

For a brief moment, her hand hovered over the access panel. She could feel her hesitation creeping in, a momentary lapse in resolve. Commander Vohr would be waiting inside, and whatever conversation they were about to have, Zyra knew it wouldn't be pleasant.

With a quiet exhale, she pressed the flesh of her palm to the panel. The door slid open with a soft hiss, revealing a dimly lit interior. The shadows stretched long in the narrow room, pooling in corners where the light didn't reach. In the centre, a table glowed with the light of holographic maps and data streams. Standing over it was Commander Vohr.

Even after all these years, his presence still managed to unsettle Zyra. He was tall, his body encased in the dark, angular armour that marked him as one of the Zarron elite. His pale skin seemed to glow faintly in the low light, but it was his eyes that truly unsettled her. They gleamed with a faint shimmer – a telltale sign of the Zarron technology fused within him. Cold, calculating eyes that saw too much, yet gave away nothing.

"Zyra," he said, his voice cutting through the silence like a blade. "You're late."

She stepped forward, keeping her posture relaxed despite the tension crackling between them.

"I didn't realise the Zarrons were still sticklers for punctuality," she replied, folding her arms across her chest in an attempt to appear unfazed.

Commander Vohr's expression didn't change.

"Poor time-keeping is for those with choices," he said smoothly. "You don't have choices."

His words sent a chill through Zyra, though she refused to show it. The power dynamic between them had always been clear. She was a creation, a tool. Commander Vohr had been there since the beginning, overseeing her development. He had seen her when she was nothing but a hybrid experiment, a blend of human DNA and Zarron ingenuity. Though Zyra had carved out a life of her own in Neon Prime, Commander Vohr would never see her as more than a weapon – a weapon that now had to be activated.

"You've spent too long amongst the humans," he said, his voice sharp with disdain. "It has made you weak."

Weak. The word stung. Zyra had fought in Neon Prime's streets, protected its citizens, built a life here. Yet, in Commander Vohr's eyes, none of that mattered. She was still the Zarron sleeper agent, created to serve, never to lead a life of her own.

She met his gaze, refusing to let him see the

turmoil roiling beneath her surface.

"I'm not weak," she said, her voice steady. "I've seen more action here than you ever could behind your holo-screens."

Commander Vohr's lips curled into a sneer.

"Action? You think mingling with humans has given you strength? You are ours, Zyra. The High Command has not forgotten your purpose. And neither should you."

His words were like chains, pulling her back into the cage she had always wanted to escape. For a fleeting moment, her gaze flicked to the side, her thoughts wandering to the life she had built – the friendships she had forged, and the people she had come to care for despite herself.

"What do you want from me, Commander Vohr?" she asked, her voice low but laced with defiance. "Why now?"

Commander Vohr stepped forward, his imposing figure casting a long shadow across the room.

"The time has come for you to fulfil your

purpose," he said. "The Zarron High Command has decided it is time to take Neon Prime. The humans have grown too bold, too confident. Their time is over. You will be the key to our victory."

Zyra's stomach clenched. So this was it. The invasion. The reason she had been created. She reeled at the thought of betraying the city she had come to love, the people she had fought to protect.

"And if I refuse?" she asked, though she already knew the answer.

"You can't refuse," Commander Vohr said, his eyes gleaming with cold amusement. "You were made for this, Zyra. There are controls in place. Fail-safes. The High Command has prepared for every contingency. You are ours."

The words struck Zyra like a physical blow. She had always known that her creators had the power to pull her back into line should she stray too far. It was a shadow that had always lurked in the back of her mind, but she had hoped, foolishly perhaps, that they would never use it. But here it was, the confirmation that her hopes of freedom had always been unrealistic.

"I'll think about it," she said through gritted teeth, her fingers twitching towards her pistol.

Commander Vohr stepped closer, his presence overwhelming.

"You won't," he said, his voice a chilling whisper. "The High Command has little patience for hesitation. They will not wait long."

With that, he turned and headed for a door at the back of the room, the conversation clearly over. Zyra watched him leave. Deep down, she had known this day would come – the day the Zarrons would instruct her to carry out their vision of her ultimate purpose. But the reality of it – the thought of betraying everything she had built – was more unbearable than she had imagined it to be.

Standing alone in the dimly lit space, her thoughts spiralling, the choice before her seemed impossible: betray the humans, or defy the Zarrons and risk losing everything.

There had to be another way. There had to be.

Neon Prime

Chapter Three

The lift hummed softly as Zyra ascended towards ground level, still grappling with the conversation she'd had with Commander Vohr. His words had left a bitter undertone, and no matter how hard she tried to focus on the present, her thoughts kept circling back to that chilling phrase: *You are ours*.

The neon lights of the city flashed past the lift's glass walls as it rose towards the surface, casting streaks of colour across Zyra's pink skin. Neon Prime had always been chaotic, but now, it felt different – more volatile. Unmistakably, something had shifted all around, a sense of tension that even the ever-present sound of engines and chatter couldn't drown out.

As the lift doors opened, Zyra stepped out

into the familiar buzz of Megara Avenue. The street was crowded, as always, but the atmosphere was thick with unease. Normally, humans and Zarrons mingled here, navigating their unspoken divides with forced politeness, but today, there was a palpable tension in the way people moved. Conversations were hushed, glances were furtive, and an edge of hostility hung in the air like a blade poised to strike.

Ahead, a gathering crowd spilled into the street, their raised voices cutting through the usual din of the city. Zyra weaved through the throngs of people, her senses on high alert as she approached the disturbance. A protest: not an unusual sight in Neon Prime, though this one seemed larger, angrier.

"Human rights!" someone shouted from the front of the crowd, their voice raw with emotion.

They were holding a sign, crudely painted with the words 'End Alien Control'.

On the other side of the street, a smaller group of Zarrons stood silent but resolute, watching the humans with thinly veiled contempt. Between the two groups, enforcers had formed a barrier, their black uniforms a stark line of authority keeping the opposing factions from tearing into each other.

Zyra's communications device buzzed in her ear:

"Zyra, are you there?"

It was Dane's voice, a welcome engagement.

"Yeah, I'm here," she answered. "What's going on?"

"There's another protest forming near the power district. A group of humans and Zarrons got into it earlier. It's getting bad out here. Where are you?"

"On Megara, near the council building," she answered, her eyes scanning the growing crowd. "There's a protest here too. It's tense."

That was putting it mildly. She could feel the situation teetering on the edge of violence. One wrong move, one spark, and it could erupt.

"Stay sharp," Dane said through a burst of

static. "Things are spiralling faster than we can handle. I've got a bad feeling about this. I'll make my way up to you."

Zyra grimaced, her hand instinctively hovering near her holster. The presence of the pistol was familiar and welcome, though she didn't want to use it. Not yet. Not when the city itself felt like a powder keg waiting to explode.

She pushed her way through the crowd until she spotted Dane approaching the edge of the protest. Tall and broad-shouldered, he had a commanding presence, accentuated by the stark black uniform he wore. The fabric, sleek and imposing, seemed to absorb the light around it, making him appear as though he had emerged from the shadows themselves. A high-collared jacket fastened with silver clasps bore the insignia of his rank, and the matte shoulder plates added an air of authority. His sharp brown eyes swept over the crowd with the same perceptiveness that had made him such an excellent enforcer. When he caught sight of Zyra, he furrowed his brows in concern.

"You look shaken," he said as they neared

each other, his voice low enough for only her to hear. "Are you ok? What's going on?"

Zyra tensed. Sometimes, Dane could be too perceptive for his own good. She trusted him – far more than most – but there were limits to how much she could let him in. If he ever found out what she really was, what she had been created for...

"I'm fine," she lied, keeping her tone even. "I'm just tired."

"Tired?" Dane echoed as he folded his arms, clearly unconvinced. "We've pulled double shifts before and you've never looked like this."

"I said I'm fine," Zyra snapped, harsher than she had intended.

His frown deepened, but he didn't push it. Before either of them could say more, a shout from the crowd shattered the moment. A glass bottle sailed through the air, smashing against the helmet of another enforcer. The crowd surged forward, and Zyra reacted instinctively, stepping in front of Dane and drawing her pistol.

"Everyone stand down!" she yelled, her voice cutting through the noise.

The crowd hesitated, their momentum faltering as they took in the sight of her. For a brief moment, there was silence. The humans glared at the Zarrons across the street, their fury simmering just below the surface. The Zarrons stared back, their expressions cold and calculating, as if daring the humans to make the first move.

Zyra's communications device buzzed again, pulling her attention away:

"We've got reports of power outages in Sector Nine," a voice crackled. "Looks like sabotage."

Her stomach twisted. Sabotage. She knew what that meant. Zarron High Command were pulling strings behind the scenes, orchestrating unrest and weakening the city's infrastructure. It was all part of their larger plan to destabilise Neon Prime from within.

She swallowed hard, her thoughts racing. Zarron High Command wanted her to disable the city's defences, to leave Neon Prime vulnerable to a carefully planned invasion. But standing here, amidst the rising anger and fear, she knew she wouldn't be able to bring herself to do it.

"I don't like this," Dane muttered, his eyes darting between the humans and Zarrons. "It feels like something's about to snap."

He had no idea how right he was. Zyra squirmed inside as the discomfort of her secret pressed down on her. How much longer could she keep pretending? How much longer before Dane – and the rest of the city – realised that officially, she wasn't supposed to be on their side?

"Do you think it's going to get worse?" Dane asked, his voice quieter now, a note of deep concern creeping in.

Zyra didn't answer immediately. She couldn't. If she told him the truth, if she told him what the Zarrons had planned, it would shatter everything.

"I don't know," she finally said.

It wasn't a lie – not entirely. She didn't know what would happen next. She didn't know how much longer she could play both sides.

Dane glanced at her, his eyes searching her face for something – perhaps for some hint of the truth she was hiding.

"If something's going on, you can tell me," he said cautiously. "You know that, right? We can figure it out together."

A wave of guilt washed over Zyra. For a brief, risky moment, she wanted to tell him everything – to unload the burden of her secret, to let him shoulder some of the weight. But she couldn't. She wasn't just an enforcer. She was a Zarron sleeper agent, created to betray the very city she had sworn to protect.

"I appreciate it, Dane," she said, forcing a tight smile. "But it's nothing. Just work stress."

He didn't look convinced, but he let it go.

"Alright," he said, his tone careful. "But if you ever want to talk..."

He let the offer hang in the air before turning his attention back to the protest.

Zyra couldn't help but worry. What if Dane

already had suspicions? Perhaps another time, he would press harder. For now though, she had to keep her focus on the more immediate threat. Zarron High Command were already making their move, weakening the city from the inside.

Her communications device buzzed once more, this time with greater urgency:

"Zyra, we need backup at Sector Nine. Possible riot brewing."

She glanced at Dane, who was already moving in the other direction.

"I'll cover things here," he said. "Go."

Zyra hesitated for a moment, watching the simmering protest before turning to make her way towards Sector Nine. The city was unravelling, and she was running out of time to decide whose side she was really on.

Chapter Four

The familiar quiet of Zyra's apartment greeted her as she stepped inside, closing the door behind her with a soft click. The place was dark, lit only by the faint glow of the neon city that streamed in through the narrow blinds, casting jagged lines of light across the sparsely furnished room. She tossed her jacket onto the couch and then sat down, her body sinking into the cushions. The tension of the day clung to her like a second skin, an invisible pressure on her shoulders that refused to relent.

For a moment, she just sat there. Her robotic arm whirred softly as she flexed it, the metallic green sheen catching the light. A Zarron design, a Zarron creation. The arm was stronger than any human limb could ever be. Faster and more precise, it was perfect in every way. And yet, it felt like a shackle.

To the humans around her, the arm didn't distinguish Zyra as a Zarron. Luckily, many humans in Neon Prime sported similar cybernetic limbs. Though less advanced, the prosthetics had become a status symbol for the more affluent humans. Although for the purposes of blending in, Zyra's arm could be dismissed as just another prosthetic, the truth was painful, a reminder of what she truly was.

Zyra stood, unable to sit still any longer, and paced to the small kitchenette. She grabbed a glass from the sideboard and filled it with tap water, then took a large gulp without really tasting it. Her mind was elsewhere – back in that grim underground warehouse with Commander Vohr, back on the streets where tensions had simmered on the verge of boiling over.

Commander Vohr's words played on a loop in her mind: *You are ours.*

She slammed the glass down onto the sideboard, the sound reverberating through the empty room. She leaned against the counter, closing her eyes and trying to steady herself. No matter how hard she tried, she couldn't shake the feeling of being trapped.

The Zarrons had crafted her, moulded her for their purposes, and now they wanted to pull her back into their fold. No matter how much she wanted to resist, how much she wanted to claim the life she had built for herself, the truth was undeniable: they owned her.

Her gaze drifted towards the corner of the room where she had placed her pistol on the small coffee table. The weapon gleamed in the faint light, a constant companion that had seen her through more altercations than she could count. It had always been a tool of survival, but now, it felt like a symbol of something darker, of the choices she would soon have to make.

She had been given a direct order: disable the city's defences. If she didn't comply, someone would come for her. She knew all too well what would happen if she defied the Zarron High Command.

But how could she do it? How could she betray this city? This place had become her home, even if it wasn't perfect. Even though the people here didn't fully know her, they had accepted her as one of their own – especially Dane.

Dane. His face flashed in her mind – the concern in his eyes, the way he had seen through her attempt to deflect. He knew something was wrong. He always knew. And if he kept pressing, kept asking questions...

Zyra pushed the thought aside. She couldn't think about that now. She couldn't let herself imagine what would happen if Dane – or anyone else – discovered what she really was. She had to focus. She had to find a way out of this.

She paced back towards the window. There had to be a way to stop the Zarrons. She couldn't be the tool they wanted her to be, but she couldn't fight them directly either – not without revealing herself. Not without putting herself in the firing line.

Her robotic hand clenched into a fist, the servos humming softly as the tension coiled within her like a spring ready to snap. She was running out of time.

And then it hit her: there was someone out there who might be able to help. Someone who had always operated on the fringes, who had no love for the Zarrons or the human authorities. Someone who owed her a favour.

Sera.

Zyra hadn't spoken to Sera in months, not since she had arrested the defiant human for hacking into a corporate mainframe and skimming data off the top. Sera had been rebellious, sarcastic, and downright frustrating, but she had also been brilliant. And when Zyra had let her walk out of the detention centre uncharged, Sera had promised that she would return the favour someday.

It was now time. 'Someday' had to be today.

Zyra grabbed her communications device from the coffee table and didn't hesitate before inputting the code. She had memorised Sera's secure channel, a line untraceable and deeply encrypted.

The communications device buzzed softly as the connection was established. After a few moments, a voice crackled through, sharp and irritated:

"Who the hell is...?"

"It's Zyra," she interrupted, her voice more

urgent than she had intended. "I need a favour."

There was a long pause on the other end, followed by a dry, sarcastic laugh.

"You're kidding, right? After all this time?"

"Sera, this isn't a joke. I wouldn't be calling you if it wasn't important."

"Alright," the hacker said after another long pause, her tone slightly softer but her wariness still clear. "What kind of favour are we talking about?"

"I need to create a false signal," said Zyra, forcing herself to be concise. "Something that will make it look like Neon Prime's defence grid is down without actually disabling it. It has to be convincing enough to fool some very... tech-savvy individuals."

"You're asking for a miracle. You realise that, right? The city's defence grid is fortified like nothing else. Layer after layer of protection. If this is about..."

"I can't explain right now," Zyra cut in, her

voice tight with the strain of urgency, "but I need this, Sera."

There was a long stretch of silence, and for a moment, Zyra's pulse quickened with the fear that Sera would refuse.

"Alright," Sera finally said. "I'll help. But I'm going to need access to some serious data streams. Military-level clearance. Can you get me that?"

"I can get you what you need," Zyra confirmed.

"Good," Sera replied. "Get me that clearance, and I'll be able to route the signal through the city's sub-grids from there. It won't hold forever, but it should be enough to fool whoever's watching."

Zyra released a slow breath, the tension in her chest easing just slightly. It wasn't a perfect solution, but it was a start.

"Thank you, Sera. If you can pull this off, I won't forget it."

"You'd better not," Sera quipped.

The communication line went dead, leaving Zyra standing alone in her apartment, her mind buzzing with what had just been set in motion.

She had bought herself some time, but how much?

The thought chilled her to the bone. With a twitch of her finger, she moved the blind a little and glanced out at the cityscape, the neon lights blinking lazily as if mocking the trouble brewing beneath the surface.

She had to keep it together – not just for her own survival, but for the entire metropolis.

Chapter Five

The sky was still an inky shade of predawn when Zyra left her apartment the next morning, her thoughts dominated by the events of the previous day and the hazardous path she had committed to. Neon Prime felt quieter at this hour, the usual cacophony of the city muted. The streets were almost empty, giving her some rare and much-needed solitude.

She pulled her jacket tighter around her as she looked up at the destination looming ahead – a towering structure of cold steel and reinforced glass that stood in stark contrast to the vibrant neon colours of the rest of the city. The building was a practical, no-frills fortress.

General Karn's headquarters.

Zyra knew him as a tough, no-nonsense man who valued efficiency above all else. She had interacted with him sparingly over the years in her role as an enforcer, but now, in her need to be granted access to the city's most sensitive military data, he was the only one she could ask; she was confident that he held her in high enough regard.

At least, that was the hope.

Once inside the building, Zyra passed through multiple security checkpoints, flashing her enforcer credentials. The guards – all humans – barely glanced at her, though she could feel the occasional flicker of curiosity in their eyes as she walked past. She had a reputation in Neon Prime's military circles: efficient, reliable, and distant. It was a carefully cultivated persona, one that kept people from digging too deeply into her past or her true nature.

The headquarters buzzed with subtle activity. Soldiers and staff moved with purpose, their footsteps echoing against the metal floors as they prepared for the day's operations. Despite this, there was an underlying tension in the air – Zyra could feel it as she passed through the corridors. It was the same tension that had been growing in the city recently. Protests, sabotage, riots. Everything was unravelling faster than anyone could control.

Zyra approached General Karn's office at the end of a long, sterile hallway. His door, flanked by armed guards, was imposing but familiar. She pressed the flesh of her palm to the scanner, and after a brief pause, the door slid open with a hiss.

General Karn was sitting behind his desk, his large frame hunched over a series of holographic map projections. They displayed various sections of the city – its power grids, defence systems, and critical infrastructure. His silver hair was neatly combed back, but the deep lines etched into his face betrayed his exhaustion. When he looked up at Zyra, his eyes narrowed as he straightened himself and rolled his shoulders back.

"Enforcer Zyra," he greeted, his tone curt but not unfriendly. "What brings you here at this hour?"

Zyra stepped forward, keeping her posture relaxed but professional.

"General, I would like to discuss the recent sabotage incidents with you. I've been investigating on my end, and I believe there's something much larger at play."

"Go on," he said as he folded his arms across his broad chest.

"I've been tracking patterns," Zyra said, her voice calm and measured despite her anxiety. "The outages in the power grids, the communications failures – they aren't random acts of vandalism. They're co-ordinated. Someone is deliberately targeting key infrastructure to destabilise the city."

General Karn's eyes flickered with interest as he studied Zyra, though his face remained unreadable.

"We've suspected as much," he said. "But without proof, it's difficult to act."

"That's why I'm here," Zyra said, sharpening her tone just enough to show her conviction. "I believe I can gather that proof, but I need access – complete access – to the city's defence systems and infrastructure. If we're going to prevent an attack, we need to act now; tensions have been on the increase."

There was a long, uncomfortable pause as General Karn stared at Zyra, weighing her words with the cold, calculating precision of a military man. Finally, he nodded, though there was a cautious edge to his agreement.

"Very well," he said. "I'll grant you temporary clearance to the classified sectors. But be careful, Zyra. If what you're saying is true, we may be facing more than just a rogue faction. We may be dealing with something much worse."

You have no idea, she thought.

"I'll be careful," she said.

The discomfort of the truth pressed against her like a lead blanket. She wasn't dealing with petty saboteurs or small-time rebels. She was up against some high-ranking Zarrons, and they had far more than just sabotage on their agenda.

As she turned to leave, General Karn's voice stopped her in her tracks.

"Zyra," he said, his tone softer but still commanding. "I know the enforcers have been under a lot of pressure lately. If there's anything else going on – anything I should know about – now is the time to tell me."

Zyra paused for a second, her back still to him. For a brief moment, she considered telling him everything – about the Zarrons, about her role in their plans. But then she pushed the thought aside. General Karn wouldn't understand. And even if he did, it was too dangerous. If the military command found out about her true nature, they would end her just as ruthlessly as the Zarrons could.

"I'll let you know if I find anything else," she said, her voice steady.

General Karn didn't press further, so she took the opportunity to leave, her mind racing as she made her way back through the headquarters.

She now had the access she needed, but this was just the beginning: she would need to rely on Sera to create the false signal in a way that wouldn't draw attention to the truth.

Chapter Six

Zyra collapsed into the worn fabric of her couch, the day hanging heavy on her shoulders. Despite how her apartment was a small sanctuary, a place she could retreat to after her long shifts, the quiet of her home did little to soothe her unease. She had been distracted all day – thinking about what she had to do, about what was at stake. She had to give the Zarrons the impression that she was willing to comply.

She stared at the ceiling, tracing the cracks she had memorised over the years, trying to ground herself. But it was no use. She kept thinking back to the looming threat. Zarron High Command wanted her to disable the city's defences. It was part of the grander plan – a plan she had no intention of being a part of. Yet, she couldn't just defy them either.

Her metal fingers tapped against the armrest of the couch. She then flexed her hand, still trying to calm herself, but the tension refused to dissipate.

Her gaze drifted to the small coffee table across the room where her communications device sat, dark and silent.

Her heart pounded in her chest as she memorised the sequence for Sera's secure link, knowing that once she'd made the call, there would be no turning back.

Zyra quickly grabbed the device and sat back down to activate it. She input the code, anxiety informing her every movement. Then, the encrypted line began to connect, each second stretching into an eternity. Finally, the link crackled to life, and Sera's sharp voice broke through the static:

"Who the hell is this?"

"It's me. Zyra," she said, getting straight to the point.

There was a pause on the other end.

"I've got what you need," Zyra said, her mind flashing back to the clearance General Karn had granted her. "I'll send you the information."

"Ok. I'll get on it right away. It'll take some doing, but I'll make it look convincing enough. Whoever's watching will think the defence grid is on the brink of collapse."

"Good. Thank you. I won't forget this."

"Oh, I know you won't," Sera said, her tone a blend of humour and barely contained annoyance. "You'd better not. I'll be in touch when it's done."

The line went dead, leaving Zyra alone in the quiet once again. She placed the communications device back on the table, her fingers lingering over it for a moment longer than necessary.

There was still one more thing to do.

She grabbed the device again, her hand trembling slightly. The military-level clearance she'd leveraged would ensure Sera had access to everything she could possibly need: security codes, access points, sub-grid locations – information that would make the hack look real without actually bringing down the city's defences. She hesitated for a brief second, the shock of what she was about to do almost disabling her.

With a sharp exhale, she initiated the transfer, inputting the code that would ensure everything reached Sera's secure line. The screen flashed as the data was sent, a small confirmation appearing once the transfer was complete. She stared at it for a moment, as though the enormity of the act hadn't quite sunk in. This was it: there was no turning back now.

She set the device down gently, her hand resting on it for a final second before she stepped away.

She walked to the window, anxiously pulling the blind aside to gaze out over the sprawling city. Neon lights blinked lazily against the smog-filled sky, casting long shadows across the streets below. The city seemed so calm now, so unaware of the threat lurking just beneath the surface.

She ran a hand through her hair, sighing deeply. She wanted to relax, to let the tension melt away, but her body wouldn't co-operate. The magnitude of her situation pressed down on her in a way that felt suffocating.

She crossed the room to the small kitchenette, her steps heavy on the cold floor. She grabbed a glass from the sideboard and turned on the tap. Water rushed out, filling the glass as her fingers tensed around its smooth surface. After pausing to let the cool liquid gather, she lifted the glass and drank slowly. The water slid down her throat, but it did little to soothe the knot in her stomach. When the glass was empty, she set it down on the counter with a soft clink, exhaling a slow, deliberate breath.

Almost subconsciously, her feet carried her to her bedroom. It was a small, dimly lit space, barely furnished with a bed tucked against the far wall. She sat on the edge of the mattress, pulling off her boots one by one and dropping them onto the floor with a dull thud. Then she undressed, her movements mechanical as she continued to worry.

The soft fabric of the duvet offered little

comfort as she climbed under it to lie down. She closed her eyes, willing herself to rest, but sleep didn't come easily; she couldn't shut off her mind, which swirled with plans and an overwhelming sense of alarm. When sleep finally claimed her, it was restless – filled with fractured dreams of flickering neon lights, the threatening gaze of Commander Vohr, and an ever-present fear, not just for herself, but for the place she called home.

Chapter Seven

Zyra stirred as the faintest hint of light seeped in through the blinds. The sun hadn't yet risen, and the quiet of predawn hung in the air like a blanket over the city. She blinked her eyes open, groggy from a restless night. Her body felt heavy and her head was slow to catch up. She lay there in a daze, staring at the ceiling as she tried to gather her thoughts for the day ahead.

She remembered that it was her day off today – a reprieve, albeit a small one. Her thoughts drifted, unfocused, swirling between the pressure she was under and the overwhelming exhaustion. She closed her eyes again, forcing herself to breathe deeply.

She was mentally and emotionally drained. She needed more sleep. The world could wait for a few more hours, at least.

She rolled over, shifting into a more comfortable position as her body relaxed into the mattress. Finally, she felt the pull of a better sleep creeping in at the edges of her mind, her breathing slowing as her muscles began to unwind.

Just as she was on the verge of drifting more deeply, a loud bang echoed through the apartment.

Her eyes snapped open. For a moment, she wasn't sure if she had imagined the intrusive noise. The room was still, silent once more. She lay there, listening, holding her breath.

Then it came again: three rapid knocks, urgent and forceful.

Zyra shot up in bed. Someone was at the door, and whoever it was, they weren't messing about. She swung her legs over the edge of the mattress and clumsily scrambled to get dressed. The bad feeling in her gut settled like a stone as she headed for the door. She didn't really want to answer it, but she couldn't afford to draw attention – not from her neighbours, and definitely not from anyone who might suspect her involvement with the Zarrons. Whatever this was, it couldn't be good.

She flung the door open, shocked at the sight before her. A figure stood in the dim light of the hallway, their face obscured by an oversized hood and mask wrapped tightly around their head. The person's posture was rigid, almost nervous, and for a split second, Zyra's instinct told her she should slam the door shut.

"Let me in," the figure said, their voice muffled by the mask, but unmistakable.

Zyra's tension eased just slightly. It was Sera. Reluctantly, she gestured for Sera to come in, and then swiftly closed the door.

Immediately, Sera pulled off the heavy hood and mask. Her look was unmistakable, even in the dim light of the apartment. Her small nose ring glinted in the soft glow of the city filtering in through the blinds, and the sharp, pretty features on her face were framed by choppy black hair streaked with purple, the sides shaved and slicked back. She wore a leather jacket studded with metal spikes over a ripped black shirt. With a huff of irritation, she stomped across the floor in her heavy boots, each step landing with a solid, defiant thud.

Zyra stared at her, still trying to process the fact that Sera knew where she lived.

"How do you know where I...?"

"All part of being a hacker," Sera said, waving a hand dismissively as she plonked herself down onto Zyra's couch. "We need to talk. Now."

Zyra's nerves were on edge. It was bad enough that Sera knew where she lived, but the urgency in her voice was alarming. Zyra crossed her arms, trying to steady her voice.

"What are you doing here? How did you even...?"

"There's been a problem," Sera interrupted, cutting Zyra off as she leaned forward, her expression serious. "A big one. I did the hack like you asked, but... it didn't go smoothly."

"What do you mean?" Zyra asked, her chest tightening.

Sera sighed, leaning back as she ran a hand through her hair.

"I managed to carry out the hack. For the next forty-eight hours, the city's defence grid will look like it's been compromised. But after that, there's a strong likelihood the illusion's going to wear off. There's nothing I can do about that. That's not the only thing. As I was working, I ran into glitches. Too many glitches. More than there should've been."

"Glitches?"

"Yeah," Sera said, her eyes narrowing. "At first, I thought it was just bad luck. But then I started thinking... why were you asking for a hack this complicated in the first place? It didn't add up. So I dug a little deeper. And I found out something, Zyra."

Zyra felt her stomach drop. The room seemed to close in around her as she waited for Sera to continue.

"You're a Zarron," Sera said, her voice hard and cold.

This time, Zyra thought better than to ask how Sera had figured this information out – Sera was brilliant, clever, *calculating*. Still though, knowing that Sera had uncovered her deepest secret, the one thing she had tried so hard to keep buried, sent her reeling.

"I know you were built for one purpose," Sera continued, her tone accusatory. "To blend in with the humans. You're under pressure to weaken the city's defences for the Zarrons. And now you've dragged me into this mess."

"Sera, I..."

"Shut up," Sera snapped, standing up and pacing the room. "You've put me in danger, Zyra! Do you even realise what kind of heat I could be under if this gets out? I've hacked into the city's defence grid to help a Zarron who's prepped for war against the humans! If this information falls into the wrong hands, we're both screwed."

"I didn't have a choice," Zyra said, clenching her fists in frustration.

Sera stopped, her eyes blazing.

"You think I care about your choices? Normally, I'd deal with someone who betrayed me like this in a more... brutal way. Unfortunately though, we're both in this together now."

"What do you mean?" Zyra asked, mentally scrambling for a solution.

Sera's anger faded slightly to be replaced by a look of genuine concern.

"When I ran into those glitches, I started thinking: this isn't just me against the system. Someone higher-up might already be on to our hack. Whether I was being intercepted by humans or Zarrons, the bottom line is this: potentially, we are both somebody's target."

Zyra's legs felt weak. She sank into the couch.

"I don't know what to do," she muttered.

Sera, despite her hardened exterior, softened slightly. She crouched down in front of Zyra, meeting her gaze with an earnest intensity.

"Look, I hate the authorities," she said, her

voice low. "You know that. But right now, our best chance might be to ask for protection from the human higher-ups in Neon Prime."

"No. I can't," said Zyra, horrified. "If they find out I'm a Zarron, that I've been lying to them for all this time, they'll never help me. I've been working undercover for years. If they think I'm part of a plot to bring the city down..."

"Think about what could happen if you *don't* ask for protection," said Sera, her expression darkening. "The Zarrons will figure you out soon enough. They'll come for you – and that's if they haven't got someone out for you already. Maybe they know something, maybe they don't; but I'm telling you, Zyra, if you don't act now, it's going to be too late."

Zyra's pulse thudded in her ears. She felt trapped – between the Zarrons and the humans, between the life she had built and the mission she had been created for. No matter how she looked at this, the walls were closing in.

"I'm not saying I want to do this," Sera continued, standing up, "but it's our best option. The authorities won't be thrilled about helping you – you'll have to come clean with them if we're going to do this right, but if we can convince them that we're both in danger, that you don't truly want to disable Neon Prime's defences and leave it wide open for the Zarrons, then they might protect us. At least give yourself a chance."

Zyra's chest tightened. The thought of going to the human authorities – of revealing what she really was and of how she had already betrayed their trust – sent a feeling of bleak terror coursing through her. However, Sera's logic was sound: if the Zarrons were on to them anyway, which was entirely plausible, there would be no escape.

Zyra cursed herself under her breath, replaying her meeting with Commander Vohr. She had let her defiance slip – she had *questioned* him. Of all the mistakes she could have made, challenging Commander Vohr's authority to his face was the most foolish. What had she been thinking? The subtle flicker of contempt in his cold, overbearing gaze should have warned her immediately. How could she have been so careless? He had probably seen right through her, sensed her hesitation towards his order.

"We need to go now, Zyra," Sera urged, her voice firm. "Before it's too late."

Feeling especially vulnerable, Zyra looked up at Sera. To go along with her was the only option. Nodding slowly, Zyra stood, her legs still shaky beneath her.

"Ok," she said quietly. "Let's go."

Chapter Eight

Zyra struggled to control her feeling of panic as she and Sera approached the military headquarters. The imposing building loomed ahead, just as cold and severe as it had been the last time she had walked its halls, but this time was different. This time, she wasn't here as an enforcer. This time, she was walking in as a traitor – or at least, that's how it felt.

Beside Zyra, Sera walked with her usual confidence, her sharp eyes scanning the area for threats. She hadn't said much since they had left Zyra's apartment, and Zyra knew why. Sera hated this plan – hated the very idea of asking the authorities for help – but they were out of options. If they didn't act now, there'd be nowhere to hide.

Zyra's feet felt like lead as she passed through the entrance, Sera now trailing just behind. The familiar security checkpoints barely registered with Zyra as she flashed her credentials, the guards' gazes shifting curiously to the visitor following her. With a sharp nod, Zyra signalled that they were together, silencing any hesitation. Her pulse raced as each step carried her closer to the one person she was now dreading to see: General Karn.

When they reached the final checkpoint, Zyra had to force herself to breathe. Sera gave her a sidelong glance, as if sensing the panic rising within her.

"You ok?" she asked, her voice low but tinged with impatience.

"No," Zyra said, swallowing hard as she pressed her palm against the security scanner. "But you're right: we don't have a choice."

The heavy door slid open to reveal the stark interior of General Karn's office. Zyra avoided making eye contact as she and Sera entered. General Karn was sat at his desk, the flickering lights of its display casting deep shadows on his face. His silver hair caught the glow, but it was the hard line of his jaw that drew Zyra's attention.

As the door closed behind them with a soft hiss, Zyra stood frozen for a second. It was Sera's nudge that brought her back to reality, forcing her to approach the desk.

"General Karn," Zyra said, her voice tight with nerves.

She consciously stood at attention, fighting the urge to shrink into the shadows. Sera, of course, had no such reservations. She crossed her arms, slouching to one side with an air of irritation.

General Karn finally looked up, his piercing eyes locking onto Zyra. His gaze flicked to Sera briefly before settling back on Zyra, suspicion darkening his expression.

"Enforcer Zyra," he said, his voice sharp. "Is everything ok?"

Zyra opened her mouth, but the words lodged in her throat. She had prepared for this moment – had rehearsed what to say on the way here – but now, standing before General Karn, it all felt hollow. How could she possibly explain what she had done?

Sera sighed loudly, rolling her eyes.

"Are you going to tell him, or should I?"

Zyra shot Sera a glance before turning back to General Karn.

"General, I..." she uttered. "I've made a mistake."

"A mistake?" he echoed, his expression hardening.

This was it: the moment Zyra had been dreading. She had to make General Karn understand, had to swallow every ounce of pride she had left.

"I... I'm a Zarron," she blurted.

The words felt foreign in her mouth after so many years of pretending. She hated the sound of them, hated what they meant.

"I was created to infiltrate, to blend in. Zarron High Command have tasked me with disabling the city's defences. They want me to make Neon Prime vulnerable to them."

Silence stretched across the room, thick and unpleasant. General Karn clenched his jaw as he balled his hands into fists on the desk.

"And yet," he said slowly, dangerously, "Neon

Prime is still standing. Why?"

"Because I don't want to see the Zarrons bring the city to its knees," Zyra said firmly. "I can't go through with following their order."

"You lied to us," said General Karn, his voice low and his disgust palpable as he briskly stood up. "All this time, you've been pretending to be human, while all along, you – a Zarron – were planning our downfall."

"Please, you have to believe me," Zyra begged, trembling as she stepped closer, desperation creeping into her tone. "Yes, I was created for that purpose – to infiltrate, to weaken Neon Prime from the inside. But I'm not behind this. I don't want to follow their orders. When the directive came to disable the city's defences, I realised I couldn't do it. I've lived among humans for so long; I don't have the hatred for them that Zarron High Command carries... I couldn't betray Neon Prime. I may have been created Zarron, but it doesn't mean I'm truly with them. I know there's no excuse for what I've done, lying to you for all these years when you've entrusted me to protect the city. But please, I'm not asking for forgiveness, I'm asking for protection."

"You have some nerve to come here asking for that," General Karn said, seething with anger.

"Look," Sera said bluntly. "Yeah, Zyra is Zarron, and yes, she has lied to you, but she didn't do what they asked. She could have handed the city over to them, but she hasn't. They probably want her dead now. That's why we're here. We're both in danger."

General Karn turned his gaze to Sera, scrutinising her with the same intensity he had given Zyra.

"What is your involvement in this?" he asked distrustfully.

"I'm just the hacker that Zyra roped into this. She was so scared of defying Zarron orders that she asked me to create a false signal to make it look like she had willingly disabled the city's defences. So yeah, if you think the Zarrons won't come after me, you're kidding yourself."

General Karn ground his teeth together as he considered their words. The relative silence was oppressive as Zyra waited for his response. She didn't dare move, didn't dare speak, anticipating that one wrong word would tip the scales against her.

Finally, after what felt like an eternity, General Karn exhaled sharply and sat back down. He looked at Zyra, his eyes hard but thoughtful.

"If you truly wanted the Zarrons to take over Neon Prime, you could have enabled them," he said, his voice rough with restrained outrage. "You had the access. You had the opportunity. And yet, you didn't. That doesn't absolve you of your initial deception, but still..."

Zyra could hardly believe it. Was he considering granting them protection? Was there still a chance?

General Karn leaned forward, his gaze unrelenting.

"You must understand, Zyra, that if I agree to offer you protection, it will not be for your sake alone. It will be because keeping you out of Zarron hands is most likely essential for the safety of the entire metropolis. You're a risk. Both of you are."

Zyra nodded, unable to speak. She had never felt so small, so powerless.

"There is a facility beneath this headquarters," said General Karn, his expression softening just slightly, though the steel in his voice remained. "It's a classified location, known to only a few. You will be moved there – both of you. It's underground, closely guarded, and completely off the grid. No one will find you, and you'll remain there until we determine how best to handle this situation."

Zyra exhaled, relief washing over her, though a sense of trepidation still lingered. She had asked for protection and been granted it, but at what cost?

General Karn stood again, his posture stiff.

"You will be kept under strict surveillance, and should anything else come to light, I will not hesitate to take further action. Do you understand?"

"Yes, sir," Zyra said quietly.

"Good," he said coldly. "I'll have someone escort you to the facility."

Chapter Nine

Zyra and Sera were led through a narrow, dimly lit corridor beneath General Karn's headquarters. The walls were cold, thick steel, reinforced with layers of concrete. There was no mistaking the sensation of being trapped underground, the sound of each footstep muted in the confined space. Two guards marched silently ahead of Zyra and Sera, their boots a deadened thud against the floor, while two more trailed closely behind the pair.

Zyra's chest tightened at the situation. The air was heavy, damp, and carried the scent of old metal and something faintly sterile. Her enhanced senses picked up every little sound – the hum of distant machinery, the soft clicks of the guards' weapons. The deeper they went, the more oppressive the environment became. Dark, claustrophobic, and guarded at every turn. She stole a glance at Sera, who had been quiet for the entire walk. Sera's expression was set, her usual bravado tempered by the tension hanging over them.

Finally, they arrived at their destination. The guards opened a large reinforced door, revealing a small windowless room furnished with only two bunks and a plain metal table. The walls were bare, and the lighting was minimal but harsh. The air was cooler, as though the very atmosphere itself had been stripped of warmth.

Zyra and Sera stepped inside, and the door closed with a heavy clang behind them. The sound caused Zyra to shudder uncomfortably. This was it: no more running, no more evading Commander Vohr and the Zarron High Command. They were locked in, isolated, and completely cut off from the outside world.

Zyra instinctively attempted to engage her neural interface, curious to see if incoming messages would be able to reach her. But nothing. Just static. She wasn't surprised – down here, communication of any kind seemed impossible. General Karn must have made sure of it.

"We're stuck," Sera muttered as she threw herself onto one of the bunks. "No tech, no way to contact anyone. Might as well be buried alive."

Zyra sat down on the edge of the opposite bunk, her hands resting limply in her lap. She stared at the floor, trying to keep her thoughts from spiralling. She had hoped that coming here would provide some form of relief, but now that they were inside, the reality of their situation was worse than she could have imagined. They were prisoners in all but name, trapped underground with no means of escape if things were to go wrong with General Karn.

"I can't believe we're here," Zyra said weakly, more to herself than to Sera.

"I get it," said Sera, rolling over and staring at the ceiling. "This feels like a defeat. We've gone from wanting protection, to being locked up like rats."

Zyra didn't answer. The silence between them

stretched on, thick with frustration and unease. As the minutes turned into hours, neither of them said a word. Uncertainty loomed over them. They had no idea what was happening above ground. They didn't even know if they could trust General Karn to keep them safe – not after the betrayal Zyra had admitted to.

The hours passed slowly. Zyra barely moved from her spot on the bunk, her mind cycling through endless worries. She had trusted General Karn enough to have requested protection, but that trust felt thinner with every second. Was this protection, or was it a calculated way of keeping them under control?

The heavy door opened, a welcome reprieve from the tedium, and a guard entered with a tray of food. He placed it on the table without a word, and then stepped back out of the small room, locking the door behind him.

Sera sat up, eyeing the tray with mild interest.

"Huh," she said, lifting one of the metal plates. "Not as bad as prison food, but it's pretty clear that Karn's not rolling out the welcome mat for us."

Zyra forced a half-smile, though her head was elsewhere. The bland meal – protein slop and some form of processed vegetables – was edible, but it did little to improve her mood. They ate in silence, the feeling of isolation sinking in further.

Just as they were finishing their meal, the sharp blare of an alarm suddenly wailed overbearingly through the small room. Zyra's heart stopped for a moment before her training kicked in. She recognised the sound straight away. It was a breach alarm – a signal that something, or someone, had broken through the main building's security.

She looked at Sera, who had already jumped to her feet, her eyes wide and unsure.

"What the hell is that?" Sera shouted, glancing around as though the walls might suddenly close in on them.

Zyra barely heard her. Breach alarms meant one thing: an imminent threat. And in a place like this, the only threat that made sense was the Zarrons.

Loud voices filtered through the door as the

guards outside exchanged quick, urgent words. Zyra strained to listen:

"The Zarrons... they've breached the building... headquarters are under attack..."

Zyra's blood ran cold. Did Commander Vohr know her whereabouts?

"What's happening?" Sera pressed.

"The Zarrons," Zyra confirmed. "They've broken into the headquarters."

"Great," said Sera, pacing the small room. "Just great. So what now? We're sitting ducks down here."

Before Zyra could answer, the door swung open. One of the guards rushed in, his face tight with panic. He motioned for them to follow.

"Come on," he said briskly. "We need to move. We've received word that there may be a bomb planted somewhere in the building. Standard protocol is to evacuate all personnel, including those under protection. We can't risk staying down here."

Zyra's heart skipped a beat. A bomb?! If the Zarrons breaking in wasn't bad enough, there was now the very real possibility that the entire building was rigged to blow.

"So where are we going?" Sera asked, her voice higher than usual, betraying her horror at the situation.

"To the surface," said the guard. "Follow us and don't fall behind."

Zyra exchanged a quick glance with Sera. They had gone underground in the hope of protection, but now they were right back where they started – in danger, running for their lives.

With a deep breath, Zyra nodded and followed the guard out into the narrow hallway. Whatever safety this underground facility had promised was gone. Now, everything rested on the storm brewing above.

Chapter Ten

Zyra and Sera moved quickly, following the guards through the narrow passageways as they made their way towards ground level. The atmosphere was tense, the guards speaking in clipped tones, their faces set in stone.

Then, as if from nowhere, a deafening blast reverberated through the underground tunnels, louder than anything Zyra had ever heard. It felt as though the very earth above had been ripped apart. Her stomach lurched as the ceiling shuddered violently. Dust and debris cascaded down, filling the air with choking clouds of grit. The overhead structures groaned in protest, with chunks of rock breaking loose as the tunnel threatened to collapse.

This wasn't just a distant explosion – something above ground had been obliterated, and the shockwave had ripped through the subterranean level.

The guards, who up until that point had moved with military precision, faltered. One stumbled, his eyes wide with panic. Before Zyra could process what was happening, everyone broke rank. They scattered in blind terror, fleeing down different passageways, their duty to escort her and Sera no longer a priority.

"Hey!" Sera shouted after them.

It was no use. The guards were gone, lost in the chaos.

Zyra stared at the last of the retreating figures, disbelief washing over her. The very people who were supposed to protect them had abandoned them.

"We have to keep moving!" she shouted, grabbing Sera's arm and pulling her down one of the tunnels.

Sera didn't protest. She followed closely as they wove through the darkened corridors. The ceiling above them continued to rumble, distant crashes echoing through the maze-like underground. Zyra quickly tried to recall the expansive layout of the building's ground level. She knew the underground network connected to several points within the headquarters, but with the guards gone, it was up to her to navigate.

Every passageway looked the same, but she pushed forward, relying on her instincts. After what felt like an eternity, they reached a narrow staircase and began their climb towards ground level.

They emerged into a part of the headquarters that Zyra recognised immediately – an old operations room used for secondary communications during drills. It hadn't been touched by the explosion, which seemed to have occurred on the opposite side of the building. The room was eerily quiet, the faint hum of machines the only sound cutting through the silence.

Zyra paused, listening for signs of life, but there was nothing. She moved to the console in the centre of the room, her fingers deftly manipulating the controls as she logged into the communications system.

"What are you doing?" Sera asked anxiously.

"We need information," Zyra replied, her focus entirely on the screen. "After everything that's happened, we can't just run out there blind."

The system soon began to display a series of encrypted messages and live feeds. A sinking feeling gripped Zyra as the full extent of the situation became clear. General Karn's forces were engaged in a fierce battle against the Zarron army. The invaders had breached the headquarters, and the surrounding streets just beyond had become one of many battlegrounds.

She watched as reports streamed in – Zarron ships had landed on the outskirts of the city. Civilians were caught in the fray.

"They've already begun," Zyra muttered in a grim tone. "It looks as though General Karn's forces are spread thin. They're barely holding their own."

Her hands clenched the edge of the console. She could only assume that Zarron High Command had decided to attack Neon Prime despite her unwillingness to help.

Just then, a familiar sensation surged through her head. She froze as a sharp pressure pulsed in her neural interface. It was a message – something she could receive now that she was no longer underground and surrounded by technological restrictions.

She recognised the signal immediately. It was Commander Vohr. His voice slid into her mind, clipped and deliberate:

"Zyra, it's not too late. Return to your purpose. Honour your duty. Do right by your Zarron creators and you will be rewarded accordingly. If you continue to resist, you and your little hacker friend will be met with suffering beyond your imagination. You can still have everything, Zyra. All you have to do is stop running."

Zyra's blood ran cold. She fought to steady herself, gripping the console as if it might anchor her.

"Zyra?" Sera asked urgently, stepping forward. "What's happening?"

Zyra blinked, shaking her head as she tried to block out the voice in her mind.

"It's Commander Vohr," she said, her mouth dry. "He's trying to..."

She couldn't finish the sentence. The fear that had been creeping up on her since the moment she'd betrayed Zarron High Command was now threatening to overwhelm her completely. She had known they would come for her, but hearing Commander Vohr's voice in her head again, feeling his influence over her, made it all too real.

"What's he saying?" Sera demanded.

"He wants me to stop resisting," Zyra said shakily. "He's promising that if I obey, we won't be hurt. But if I don't... he'll destroy us."

Sera's lips pressed into a tight line, her anger barely contained.

"You know that's a lie," she insisted. "He's going to come for us no matter what. We're in too deep now."

Zyra nodded, trying to shove the panic down. She couldn't let Commander Vohr control her. She couldn't betray the humans – not after they had been so easy to live with overall.

"We have to move," Sera urged, her voice pulling Zyra back to the present. "We can't stay here."

Zyra nodded, shaking off the last remnants of Commander Vohr's message. She pulled up a map of the building, her hands almost steady as she zoomed in on a route that would lead them outside, but not into the worst of the danger.

"We'll head this way," she said, pointing to the screen. "It will take us to an exit close to the transport bay."

Sera nodded, already at the door, her jaw set in determination.

Chapter Eleven

The night sky over Neon Prime was thick with smoke and the glow of distant fires. Zyra and Sera hurried through the dim streets, the towering buildings casting long, eerie shadows. When they finally reached the transport bay, Zyra felt a wave of relief wash over her as they stepped into the quiet docking area. It was still. The fighting hadn't reached this part of the city yet.

"We should be safe here for a little while," she muttered, scanning the area.

Dozens of stationary hover-cars were parked in neat rows, their sleek, streamlined bodies gleaming under the faint light. No one else was around, and for the first time in hours, the quiet emptiness offered a rare moment of calm.

"Let's hide there," Sera suggested, pointing at a gap between two larger vehicles.

They slipped into the space, crouching low. Zyra knew they couldn't stay here forever, but it was still a welcome reprieve in the circumstances.

Before she could properly catch her breath, she caught the sound of people shouting in the distance, the cacophony growing louder by the second. Her instincts kicked in immediately, her body becoming rigid.

"Do you hear that?" she whispered.

"Yeah," Sera replied, just as quietly, listening intently. "Sounds like a fight."

The noise wasn't just getting louder; it was heading straight towards them, carrying the unmistakable sound of a brawl, of fists striking flesh.

"Zarrons and humans," Zyra whispered, recognising the distinct cadence of Zarron combat techniques in the mix.

The fight was moving fast, and it wouldn't be long before it reached their hiding spot.

"Time to go," Sera said, already preparing to run.

Zyra nodded, about to follow when a voice cut through the din.

"Help!"

It was faint but unmistakable, the sound of someone calling out in pain. Zyra froze. She knew that voice. Dane.

"Zyra, we need to go," said Sera, tugging at her arm.

"It's Dane," Zyra said, her voice shaking as her eyes darted in the direction of the sound. "He's in trouble."

"We need to worry about ourselves," Sera said bluntly.

Zyra clenched her fists, torn between the instinct to flee and the need to help her friend. Dane had been her work partner for years – loyal, reliable, and kind. He'd always had her back, always trusted her without question. She couldn't leave him, not now.

"I can't just run," Zyra said, determination flooding through her. "I have to help him."

Before Sera could argue, Zyra darted out from their hiding place, rushing towards the sound of the fight. She weaved through the smoke, her enhanced senses guiding her.

And then she saw him – Dane, struggling to stand, a deep wound on his leg, barely able to keep the advancing Zarrons at bay. His expression was ashen. His movements were sluggish and pained.

"Dane!" Zyra shouted as she ran to him.

He snapped his head up, his eyes widening in recognition. Relief flashed across his face, but it was quickly replaced by agony as he clutched his injured leg.

"Zyra... help..."

Without thinking, Zyra darted over and scooped him up, the enhanced Zarron strength of her robotic arm functioning effortlessly as she lifted his weight. Dane's brows shot up in disbelief, but there was no time for questions. She carried him with ease, running as fast as she could towards a quieter part of the city, Sera sprinting alongside them.

They ducked into an alleyway several streets away, where the noise of the brawl faded into the background. Zyra gently set Dane down against a wall, her chest heaving as she caught her breath.

"Dane," she said softly, kneeling beside him, "we're going to help you."

Sera crouched down, assessing his injury.

"It's bad, but not critical," she said. "We just need to stop the bleeding."

Dane winced but managed a smile.

"Zyra... You lifted me... Like I weighed nothing."

Zyra froze, her hands stilling on his leg. She glanced at Sera, whose face was impassive, waiting to see how this would play out.

Dane's eyes, full of pain and confusion, locked onto Zyra's.

"How the hell did you...?" he said before pausing, realisation dawning on his face. "You're a Zarron?!"

A feeling of bleakness quickly settled over Zyra. The one truth she had been hiding from Dane, the truth that could shatter everything, was now laid bare. She swallowed, the words almost refusing to come.

"I'm sorry," she said, her voice strained with desperation. "I never meant to lie to you. I'm not your enemy, I swear. Please... please believe me."

For a long moment, Dane just stared at her, his expression unreadable. Then, to her surprise, he shook his head, letting out a soft, almost incredulous laugh.

"You're not an enemy, Zyra."

Zyra blinked, caught off guard by his reaction.

"Look..." Dane said, wincing as he shifted his weight a little. "I don't know the full story here, and I don't need to. All I know is that I've never felt anything but safe with you.

Hell, I feel safe now, with you helping me... Whatever mess you're in, it doesn't change who you are to me."

He glanced down at his leg and then back at her, his gaze softer now. Zyra hadn't realised just how much she had needed to hear those words.

"Thank you," she said, her tone loaded with raw emotion.

Zyra and Sera worked quickly, cleaning and bandaging Dane's leg with what little they had. Once they had finished, he let out a sigh of relief.

Just as a brief moment of calm was beginning to settle over them, Dane's communications device buzzed to life. He frowned, tapping the device on the side of his ear to listen in.

"It's General Karn," he mouthed to Zyra, his face tightening with concentration.

He was quiet for a few moments, and then nodded grimly. As soon as the message ended, he turned back to Zyra, his expression serious.

"General Karn wants to see you," he said. "He says that if I happen to see you, I'm supposed to tell you to meet him at Sublevel Nine, Sector C – an underground bunker."

"Tell him I'm on my way," she said.

Dane nodded dutifully.

"You'd better stick with me," Zyra told Sera. "It's probably your best chance of survival."

"Yeah, I figured," said Sera, still not sounding pleased about the situation, but accepting of it nonetheless.

Zyra turned back to Dane. She hesitated; she didn't want to leave him, but she knew what had to be done.

"Dane, you should go. You'll be safer on your own. Trust me: you don't want to get mixed up in what I'm involved with."

He gave her a small, reassuring smile.

"Zyra, whatever you're caught up in, I know you'll do the right thing," he said. "Take care of yourself, ok?"

"You too, Dane. Stay safe."

As Dane leaned heavily on Zyra and Sera for support, they helped him to his feet, their arms wrapped around him to steady his wavering balance. He grimaced, his pain still evident as he attempted to put weight on his leg. With a laboured breath, he took a tentative step, and then began limping, out of the alley and away into the quiet distance. Zyra watched him until he rounded a corner, deeply concerned for his struggle.

"Let's go," she said, turning to Sera. "General Karn will be waiting for us."

Chapter Twelve

Zyra and Sera descended into the depths of the underground bunker, the faint hum of machinery echoing against the metallic walls. The air was cool, but the small space was oppressive, and with each step, Zyra's nerves tightened like a coiled spring. General Karn had called for her, but she wasn't sure what kind of reception awaited. After everything – the lies, the betrayal, the Zarron identity she had kept hidden for so long – what would he have to say?

When they reached the bottom of the stairwell, Zyra and Sera were led by two guards through a series of narrow corridors. Stopping in front of a sturdy reinforced door, the guards stood aside as it slowly slid open to reveal a small room. General Karn stood at the far end, a holographic map of Neon Prime's current battle zones flickering in front of him. He looked up as Zyra and Sera entered, his expression unreadable.

Bracing herself for the worst, Zyra reluctantly stepped forward with Sera close beside her. Would General Karn arrest them on the spot? Could she blame him if he did?

For a long moment, he said nothing, simply observing them with a calculating gaze.

"Zyra," he said finally, his voice level but with no warmth. "You've put me in a difficult position."

Zyra swallowed hard, nodding.

"I understand that, sir."

"I don't think you do," General Karn said as he stepped around the holographic map, approaching them slowly. "You've lied to your colleagues. You've lied to me. You've lived among us, worked with us, all whilst hiding the truth of what you really are."

Zyra's chest tightened. This was exactly the confrontation she had been afraid of.

"I had no choice. The Zarrons..."

"I don't care about your reasons," General Karn interrupted, his tone firm but not unkind. "What I care about is where your loyalties lie now. That's the only thing that matters."

"My loyalties are here," Zyra insisted as she met his gaze and spoke decisively. "To Neon Prime. I've refused to help the Zarrons – refused to carry out the mission they gave me. I'm not their puppet anymore."

General Karn studied Zyra for a moment longer.

"Good," he said assertively. "Because I'm prepared to offer you a deal."

"A deal?" Zyra repeated, caught off guard.

"If you agree to fully co-operate with me – if you give me everything you know about Zarron operations, their weaknesses, their tactics – I'll ensure your protection. I'll make sure the Zarron High Command can't get to you, and that the humans don't retaliate against you for your past. But it means you must cut ties with Zarron High Command completely. No more playing both sides. You need to betray them, once and for all."

The offer was exactly what Zyra needed – protection, a way out – but it also meant crossing a line she could never return from. If she agreed, there would be no more room for conflicted feelings. Although she had been created by the Zarrons and had always considered that to be a core part of her identity, she'd be burning that bridge for good.

However, as she stood there, thinking of everything that had happened – the fact that the Zarrons had used her, had tried to manipulate her, and had wanted her to betray Neon Prime – the anger bubbled up inside, hotter than ever. She was done with being their tool. The Zarrons had created her, yes, but they had never cared about her, only about what she could do for them.

"I accept your offer, General Karn," Zyra said formally, her voice steady. "I'll give you everything I know."

General Karn's expression softened just slightly, as though he had been expecting this response but had wanted to hear it. He turned to address Sera, who had been watching the exchange in silence.

"And you," he said. "You're in this too now. You've been involved in a serious hacking operation, but I don't take pleasure in punishing people when there is another way. If you co-operate and use your skills to help us, you'll receive the same protection as Zyra. You'll be safeguarded from the Zarrons, and I'll make sure no human authorities come after you for your past activities. But understand this: the slightest hint of betrayal from either of you, and the consequences will be severe."

Sera looked at Zyra, then back at General Karn, weighing the offer.

"I'm in," she said. "You would be right in thinking that I didn't want to get tangled up in any of this, but as it stands, if it's a choice between working with you versus getting killed by Zarrons, I'll take my chances on your side."

"Good," said General Karn, satisfied. "Now, listen carefully. We don't have much time."

He moved back to the holographic map. Zyra and Sera followed. The three of them studied the glowing layout of the city. He then tapped a section of the map, prompting it to zoom in and show the Zarron-occupied sectors of Neon Prime.

"We've managed to gather some intelligence that Commander Vohr himself is leading the Zarron assault. He's set up a command centre in the heart of their territory at the far end of the city. We believe he's overseeing the entire operation from there."

Zyra's stomach twisted at the mention of Commander Vohr's name. She had wondered whether something like this might be the case, but hearing it confirmed filled her with an overwhelming sense of dread.

"We're planning a co-ordinated strike," General Karn continued. "We can't afford to let Commander Vohr consolidate his forces. We need to take out his command centre and cause as much disruption as possible. Zyra, you know him better than any of us. Your knowledge of Zarron tactics will be invaluable. You'll be assigned to a small infiltration team. We'll need to get close enough to strike without drawing attention."

Zyra nodded, already running through the possible scenarios in her mind.

"I'm up for it," she said. "If we can get this right, we might just throw the whole Zarron operation into disarray."

Sera studied the map for a moment before speaking up.

"I assume you want me to use my hacking skills to disrupt their communications," she said. "I could probably cut off their internal systems, maybe cause some trouble in their ranks."

"Excellent," said General Karn. "Your skills could give us the edge we need."

Zyra felt a surge of adrenaline. This was it: her chance to make things right – to fight back against the Zarrons not as their agent gone rogue, but as someone fighting for something bigger than herself. The anger she'd felt earlier at having been used and manipulated was now fuel.

General Karn stepped back from the map, his expression stern.

"This mission is critical," he said. "If we succeed, we'll cripple the Zarrons' ability to continue their invasion. If we fail... it doesn't bear thinking about."

Zyra met General Karn's gaze, her determination hardening. He studied her for a moment, a flicker of approval in his eyes.

"Right," he said. "You leave at dawn. Get some rest."

Zyra and Sera exchanged a look as they stepped away from the map. The fight ahead of them was daunting, but for now, Zyra felt something she hadn't allowed herself to feel for a while.

Hope.

Chapter Thirteen

At the break of dawn, the sky over Neon Prime was painted with a muted haze, streaks of crimson light barely piercing through the thick atmosphere of smoke and dust. The city, once a beacon of florescent vibrancy, now sat in eerie silence as if bracing itself for the battle to come. Zyra crouched low behind a barrier, her enhanced senses scanning the shadows for any sign of movement. Her pulse thrummed in her ears, steady but heavy, each beat reminding her of the danger she faced.

Beside her, a team of high-ranking human soldiers waited, their weapons poised and ready. These weren't ordinary enforcers. They were the best of Neon Prime's military, seasoned fighters who had faced countless combat situations on other planets far away. But even they seemed tense. This mission was different. This was a strike closer to home, deep into the Zarron territory of Neon Prime.

Zyra exhaled slowly, her nerves frayed as she calculated their next move. She hadn't been trained for battle – not in the traditional sense. However, years spent as an enforcer had taught her plenty. She had learnt to adapt, to think fast, and to fight when it mattered. Though she wasn't a soldier, her time spent protecting the people of Neon Prime, albeit undercover, had sharpened her abilities.

A soldier gestured forward, and the team moved silently, slipping through the jagged ruins of the city. The low lighting and early morning shadows provided the perfect cover. Zyra's eyes scanned every corner, every darkened alley. The Zarron patrols were tight, but she could anticipate their movements.

She moved with predatory focus as they neared the Zarron command centre, a fortress of dark metal and sharp angular lines at the far end of the city. She felt the tension build as they moved in, closer to where Commander Vohr would be.

A deep unease settled in her gut. She knew the risks. This mission could end with her standing face to face with the one who had held more control over her than anyone else. The thought made her blood run cold, but she pushed it aside. She had to stay focused. There was no room for hesitation.

As they reached the edge of the compound, slipping past the final Zarron patrol, Zyra signalled to the team. The soldiers readied themselves. They were going in.

With a swift motion, the breach began. Explosives took down the outer wall, sending shockwaves through the structure. The soldiers charged in, weapons raised, as disorder erupted inside. Alarms blared throughout the building as Zarron troops scrambled to respond, but the humans moved fast, cutting through the resistance with military precision.

As Zyra fought her way through the command centre, several Zarron guards closed in around her. She dispatched them with a blend of her own raw Zarron strength and the combat skills she had honed as an enforcer. Adrenaline coursed through her veins, her movements fluid and lethal.

However, something went wrong. The human soldiers scattered, caught in a sudden onslaught of Zarron reinforcements. In the confusion, Zyra found herself separated from her team.

She pressed herself against a wall, her heart pounding in her chest. The sounds of battle raged around her, but in the narrow hallway where she stood, everything felt unnervingly quiet. Too quiet.

A cold chill ran down her spine, and she knew, even before she heard the footsteps, who was approaching.

Commander Vohr.

He appeared at the end of the corridor, his tall, imposing figure cutting a dark silhouette against the flashing emergency lights. His armour gleamed, sleek and angular. His eyes glinted with a threatening intensity; his expression was one of pure malice, his lips curling into a sneer as he regarded Zyra.

"So," he said, his voice low and venomous, "my creation has returned, only to betray me. Disgusting."

Zyra shuddered at how he had almost spat the last word. Despite her fear, she did her best to steady herself, squaring her shoulders.

"I was never yours," she said as she looked him firmly in the eyes.

"You were made to obey your Zarron master," he said, seething with rage. "I gave you life. And now here you are, turned against your own kind! How dare you?!"

"I'm not your weapon," Zyra insisted, though a feeling of dread roiled inside with each word. "Neon Prime is my home, and I'll fight to protect it."

Commander Vohr's expression darkened. In an instant, he lunged at Zyra, moving with a speed and precision that only a Zarron could.

She barely managed to dodge him, her reflexes kicking in just in time.

He struck again, his movements a blur of controlled violence. His fist whistled past her ear as she weaved, the displaced air hot against her skin. She had to block the next blow – his knuckles crashed against her forearm with enough force to make her teeth rattle. As she blocked and countered several times again, she could tell that his every grunt and snarl was powered by his fury at her betrayal.

Commander Vohr pressed forward, using his weight to trap her against the corridor's walls. His breath came harsh and ragged in her face as they grappled. When his elbow caught her ribs, the pain bloomed sharp and white-hot.

She twisted away from another crushing blow that dented the wall panel behind her, the sound of the impact drowning out her heavy breathing. His rage was making him predictable, making him sloppy. Each wild swing revealed the control he was losing – over her, over himself. Sweat stung her eyes as she ducked another attempt of his, but her resolve crystallised with each passing second. The corridor's light caught the fury in his eyes, twisting his familiar features into something monstrous.

Suddenly, he grabbed her by the throat, slamming her hard against the wall, his grip crushing her as he leaned in.

"You think you can defy me?" he growled bitterly. "You're nothing without me!"

Zyra gasped – desperately, weakly – her vision blurring as his strength threatened to suffocate her. But she wouldn't give in. With a surge of adrenaline, she twisted out of his hold, her arm locking his and forcing him back.

Then, she saw it: the moment she'd been waiting for.

He lunged at her again, but this time, she was ready. Ducking under his wild swing, she twisted, quickly freeing her pistol from its holster. The weapon was in her hand before he could react, and in one smooth motion, she spun and pulled the trigger.

The laser beam burst forth with a high-pitched whine, illuminating the corridor walls in a piercing shade of electric azure. Striking Commander Vohr's forehead, the impact snapped his neck back with blistering force. Time seemed to slow as his forward momentum carried him another half-step, his face a mask of dawning comprehension.

As the putrid smell of burnt flesh started to

overwhelm the air, he swayed on his feet, fighting a losing battle to stay upright. The hatred in his eyes flickered like a dying flame as his body betrayed him, trembling uselessly as he crashed to his knees.

"You... were... supposed to help us..." he said, his voice fading into a rasp.

With a strained gasp, he collapsed forward and struck the floor – heavy and final.

Zyra lowered her pistol and moved to stand over him, her chest heaving from exertion. The hallway was silent again, but the personal cost of the fight felt like white noise – overbearing and relentless. Whilst cuts and bruises littered her body, the emotional toll of having confronted the one who had controlled her for so long left her feeling strangely hollow.

Suddenly, her communications device buzzed. The voice of one of the human soldiers crackled through:

"Zyra, come in. Mission accomplished. The Zarrons are retreating."

Zyra let out a long breath, relief flooding

through her. As she looked down at Commander Vohr's body, a deep sense of finality settled upon her. She had fought to protect Neon Prime, but she had also fought to save herself.

And now, at last, she could be free.

With one last glance at her creator's fallen form, she turned and began making her way back to her team, ready to face whatever was in store.

Chapter Fourteen

The remains of General Karn's headquarters stood like a battered monument to survival. Much of the once imposing structure now lay in ruins, torn apart by the Zarron invasion. The air was still thick with the acrid scent of smoke and debris. Workers and soldiers moved through the rubble, their voices a low murmur as they began the long process of clearing the wreckage and restoring what had been lost. Yet, despite the devastation, there was a feeling of hope in the air – a calm after the storm.

Zyra stood near the shattered windows of what had once been a tactical room, staring out at the remnants of the city. It would take time to rebuild the physical damage and even longer to repair the scars the attack had left on the city's people, but still there was a sense of relief that the worst was over.

Behind her, she could hear the heavy footsteps of General Karn approaching. She turned to face him, her body still aching from her brutal showdown against Commander Vohr.

As he stood in the doorway, General Karn's imposing figure was silhouetted by the early morning light filtering in through the broken walls. His expression was a blend of weariness and relief, the demands of the last few days etched prominently in the lines around his eyes. When he locked his gaze onto Zyra, however, there was something else: admiration and respect.

"You did it," he said as he took a step closer to her, exhausted but sincere. "We wouldn't be standing here if it wasn't for you."

Zyra shifted uncomfortably, not quite sure how to respond. She had done what the situation had demanded, but was still grappling with the magnitude of it all.

"It wasn't just me," she said humbly. "A lot of people fought to protect Neon Prime."

"That's true," General Karn agreed, pausing for a moment as he moved to look out at the ruined cityscape. "But you turned the tide. You broke away from the Zarrons. That took more than just skill. It took bravery."

"I…" Zyra began.

"You saved this city, Zyra," he said firmly as he turned to look at her, "and for that, we owe you."

Zyra winced at his words. While she felt a measure of pride, there was also a deep, lingering discomfort at everything that had happened and what it had cost the city and its people.

"Thank you," she said, her voice low as she looked away, back out at the horizon. "But I'm not sure what happens now. For me, I mean."

General Karn studied her for a long moment before nodding slowly.

"That's why I want to talk to you," he said. "I want to make you an offer."

"An offer?" she repeated as she turned back to face him.

General Karn clasped his hands behind his

back, his posture as formal as ever despite the destruction around them.

"I want you to continue working with us. Your skills – both as an enforcer and as someone who understands Zarrons – are invaluable. I'm offering you a high-ranking position within our military, a chance to continue defending Neon Prime."

For a moment, Zyra didn't know how to respond. Part of her wanted to accept immediately – after all, she had always enjoyed working as an enforcer and had proven to herself and others that she was invested in the protection of Neon Prime. But another part of her hesitated; it wasn't a decision to be taken lightly.

"I don't know," she said honestly, her gaze becoming distant. "After everything that's happened, I think I need time to work out who I am. For so long, I've been living for others. Maybe I need to figure out what it's like to live a quieter life – one where I'm not always fighting for something."

"That's entirely understandable," said General Karn. "I won't pressure you. Take all the time you need. Just know that whatever you decide, you've earned my respect. You don't have to keep fighting if you don't want to, but you'll always have a place here no matter what."

Zyra smiled, feeling a swell of gratitude towards him.

"Thank you, sir. I appreciate that."

"There's something else I want to say," said General Karn, taking a deep breath before continuing. "I fully forgive you, Zyra: for pretending to be human, for everything. At the time, you were following orders. You didn't know any better than to do what the Zarrons commanded. But breaking away from them... that took real courage. You chose to think for yourself, to fight for something you believe in. That's what matters."

Zyra felt a lump rising in her throat, a surge of relief intertwined with a sense of closure. She had spent so long feeling guilty, trapped between two worlds, but hearing General Karn's words – his forgiveness – felt like a weight had been lifted.

"You're braver than you realise," he said, his

voice steady. "You stopped the Zarron High Command from taking over Neon Prime. That's not something that just anyone could have done."

Zyra nodded, swallowing back the emotion that threatened to surface.

"I just did what I had to do," she said.

"Sometimes, that's the hardest thing," said General Karn.

After a moment of silence, Zyra's thoughts drifted.

"How's Dane?" she asked.

"He's doing well. He'll be back to full duties soon."

"Good. He's one of the best people I know."

"He has always spoken highly of you. He'll be glad to see you."

Zyra smiled. Dane had always been good with her, even after learning the truth about her Zarron identity. Knowing he was safe and recovering was one less worry on her shoulders.

She cast her gaze over the cityscape again. The damage from the Zarron attack was evident, but beyond the ruins, it was clear that life would return to normal again. It would take time – there were buildings to repair, people to mourn, and wounds to heal – but Neon Prime had survived.

And so had she.

She felt free. The chains of her past – her life as a Zarron agent, the guilt of the lie she had lived – had finally been broken. The future was full of unknowns, but it was hers to decide now.

She didn't know where her path would lead. Perhaps she would accept General Karn's offer and continue working for Neon Prime. Or maybe she would take a step back, find a quieter life, and figure out who she really was. Whatever she chose, she knew one thing for certain: she would no longer be defined by her past.

Epilogue

Several months later, Zyra stood on the open-air observation deck of Neon Prime's central command tower, gazing out at the city she had once nearly lost. The skyline was a mixture of rebuilt structures and fresh innovations, with new hover-car routes weaving gracefully between the gleaming towers. From here, the city seemed more alive than ever, proof of its resilience and the spirit of its people.

She inhaled slowly, enjoying the cool air as it brushed against her skin. She had finally found peace – not just in the city, but within herself.

It had taken time, of course. After everything that had happened, she had needed to step away. Leaving Neon Prime, albeit briefly, had been difficult. Nevertheless, it had been necessary. Time spent away from the city had given her clarity. She had travelled to distant colonies, seeing the world through a different lens. It had reminded her of what she truly valued. Neon Prime wasn't just a city; it was her home. Its people, its energy, even its frictions – they were all a part of her.

Upon her return, she had felt rejuvenated and resolute. The time away had answered the question she had carried with her since she'd left: she wanted to stay and protect this place. And so, with newfound purpose, she had gladly accepted General Karn's offer.

Now, Zyra was a high-ranking officer within Neon Prime's military. She wasn't just an enforcer anymore; she was someone who held the responsibility to shape the future defence of the city – guiding teams, preparing strategies, and working directly under General Karn.

And she wasn't working alone.

One of the first things she had asked for upon her return to Neon Prime was for Dane to be promoted to work alongside her. General Karn had happily approved her request immediately. Dane had more than proven himself, and in his new role, he was not only excellent, but someone who Zyra could always rely on. Their partnership was as strong as ever, and the two of them could now continue working together to keep Neon Prime safe.

Zyra smiled to herself as she thought of Dane. His loyalty, his ability to immediately see beyond her Zarron origins, had helped her more than she could ever express. He had trusted her when others might have turned away, and now, in their new roles, he would continue to prove that his trust in her was well placed.

Zyra's life had changed in more ways than just her rank. She no longer hid what she was. Refusing to be ashamed of her true identity, she chose to openly live as a Zarron among the people of Neon Prime. It hadn't been an easy decision, but it was the right one. After years of hiding, of pretending, of living a double life, she was done. The humans of Neon Prime needed to see that not all Zarrons were like the ones who had attacked the city. Zyra wanted to show them that she wasn't their enemy – and neither were the countless Zarron civilians who just wanted to live peacefully within the city's borders.

To Zyra's relief, her candour went a long way towards promoting peace between the humans and Zarrons of Neon Prime. Relations between the two groups remained complicated, but thanks to her efforts, the bulk of the tension had begun to ease. Humans were more open to working alongside Zarron civilians, and Zarrons civilians, in turn, felt safer in the city they had come to call home. Zyra had helped bridge that divide, and it was a legacy she was proud of.

Naturally, not everyone had chosen the path she had. Sera had been offered a position within General Karn's intelligence team, but true to form, she had turned it down. Zyra hadn't been surprised – Sera had never been one to follow rules. Instead, Sera had thanked General Karn for the offer and promised to retire from hacking, having gained a newfound respect for the authorities she had once defied. She had seen firsthand what it took to defend the city, and while she wasn't interested in working for the authorities, she wasn't about to stir up trouble either.

Sera had forgiven Zyra for dragging her into

the situation with the Zarrons, and the two of them had parted ways on good terms. "I'm still a rebel at heart," Sera had said with a smirk, "but after everything, I wouldn't hesitate to grab a drink with you sometime."

Zyra had chuckled companionably at that. Sera had a hard edge and her own way of doing things, but it was clear they had forged a bond that wouldn't easily fade.

As she looked out over the city now, Zyra felt lighter. She no longer had to live in the shadows, no longer had to pretend to be something she wasn't. Her thoughts drifted as she watched the hover-cars moving through the sky and the people below going about their daily lives. It wasn't perfect – there was still work to be done – but it was home. She had fought to protect this city. And now, she would fight to help it grow.

As the sun began to set on the horizon, casting a warm, golden glow over the metropolis, Zyra smiled softly. She had faced down her enemies, her past, and even herself – and had come out the other side stronger.

Peace had been restored, war was no longer a looming threat, and at last, she was free.

www.ingramcontent.com/pod-product-compliance
Ingram Content Group UK Ltd.
Pitfield, Milton Keynes, MK11 3LW, UK
UKHW030723240225
455493UK00004B/309

9 781916 347823